Swavely's story is as lively and authentic as a piece of fiction can be. In just a few short lines, I felt as if I knew both the famous preacher and the famous author like brothers. This is the rare piece of non-history that feels like real history to the point of the reader feeling a part of history. How many times have we all thought, "I wish I could have been a fly on the wall when..."? With this story, you can be, and it's as glorious an experience as you thought it might be.

> Wayne Thomas Batson, bestselling author of *The Door Within* Trilogy, *The Myridian Constellation*, and *A Christian's Carol*

For those who love both Dickens and Spurgeon and wonder if they ever met—they did, as surely as any of Dickens' characters "live" in the fiber of literary culture, and as sure as Spurgeon's words make the ancient biblical stories come alive. This is a satisfying and touching account of two beloved world-changers.

> Latayne Scott, award-winning author of *A Conspiracy of Breath, The Mona Lisa Mirror Mystery*, and over 25 other books

All good fiction is based upon the premise of "What if…?" Dave Swavely's story not only has a great "what if" premise, but it makes you say to yourself, "I wish…" as in "I wish this happened." After reading this, you'll want to run to the bookshelf and spend time with both these men!

> Thor Ramsey, comedian-turned-pastor and author of several books, including *The Most Encouraging Book on Hell Ever*

Really cool! Dave Swavely has done something special in pulling two great minds into the same room for our benefit. Personalities and worldviews bump up against each other, hinting at feelings and sentiments of an age not unlike our own.

> Michael Guaglione, co-founder of Eye-Catcher Creative

This fictional but realistic conversation between the two celebrities is humorous, thought-provoking, and potentially life-changing. Seasoned author Dave Swavely keenly captures Spurgeon *and* Dickens in this page-turning narrative. An unexpected delight!

> Ray Rhodes, Jr., author of *Yours, till Heaven; the Untold Love Story of Charles and Susie Spurgeon* and *Susie: The Life and Legacy of Susannah Spurgeon.*

Words with Wings

Spurgeon meets Dickens

DAVE SWAVELY

Published by The Way With Words

1337 Greenhill Road, West Chester, PA, 19380

Copyright © 2023 Dave Swavely

ISBN: 979-8-218-23414-0

To my late friend Harry Reeder, who exhibited both
Spurgeon's holy gravitas and Dickens' cheerful wit

which is cited in *Dickens: Interviews and Recollections*, edited by Philip Collins (London: Palgrave Macmillan, 1981, p. 289). In that book a third party reports: "Spurgeon's behaviour at a German church being discussed he [Dickens] thought that Spurgeon was quite right in getting impatient over the doctrine of baptism and Heaven knew that he was no friend of Spurgeon's." That quote refers to comments Dickens made in 1860, seven years before Spurgeon started an orphanage and ten years before the encounter imagined in this story. And notice that Dickens was actually *defending* Spurgeon against the criticism of others, which may indicate a trajectory of greater respect for him.

The only other references Dickens made to Spurgeon are found in the non-fiction book he wrote with Wilkie Collins, *The Lazy Tour of Two Idle Apprentices* (1857), which was about their visit to towns in the English countryside. None of them are negative, as Dickens twice mentions Spurgeon's books being prominent in bookstores and makes one passing reference to the large crowds that attended the Metropolitan Tabernacle.

In my novel *Next Life,* from which this story is adapted, the narrator finds himself in heaven (more specifically the Intermediate State) and is sent back in time to witness a series of seemingly unrelated past events. We don't know whether people in heaven make such trips to the past, of course, but it seems possible since God exists outside of time, so I chose to depict it fictionally as a way of illustrating how heaven will be much more exciting than sitting around on clouds playing harps all day. I mention this here because it explains the references in the story to the narrator having no physical body—2 Corinthians 5 says that in the Intermediate State we will be "naked" (v. 3), "unclothed" (v. 4), and "absent from the body" (v. 8), as we await the new glorified bodies that we will receive at the final resurrection (Rev. 20:5, 13). This version of the story doesn't require an understanding of all that, however, because it can simply be read as a vivid dream that the narrator experiences.

There is no historical account of Spurgeon and Dickens meeting one another, but now there is an imaginative, fictional one based on historical facts, which are documented in the notes following the story.

1

In the immortal first words of a legendary allegory that was an inspiration to both our protagonists, "As I slept, I dreamed a dream."

A heavenly guide whom I could barely perceive ushered my bodiless soul down from above to the English countryside, and my eyeless sight followed a polished horse-drawn carriage down a lane to a large house that seemed slightly familiar to me. I could tell it was a dark night, even though the light from the oil lamps and candles on the property were exaggerated in my spiritual perception.

So were the menagerie of good and evil spirits that hovered near the stocky, bearded man who exited the coach—unbeknownst to him of course. He stepped up to the front door and was met there by a somewhat portly middle-aged woman who said, "Welcome to Gad's Hill Place, Mr. Spurgeon. Mr. Dickens is waiting for you in the library."

If I'd had a mouth and lungs, I would have gasped. But as it were, my metaphorical head started spinning, and even without lips and vocal cords, I somehow managed to ask a question of someone I couldn't see but knew was there.

Were Spurgeon and Dickens friends? I thought they never met...at least it was never recorded that they did, right?

This was the only time, someone answered. *It's*

a meeting no one knew about on June 7, 1870, two days before Dickens died.

An unseen hand guided me into the house so I could witness the encounter. My feelings of awe and glee at the time prevent me from remembering and recording exact details of the conversation between the two giants, excepting some I was able to reconstruct from related facts and written excerpts that I found afterward in the historical record. But suffice to say that the words these two men spoke to one another were almost as brilliant as theirs that can be read in print. I doubt that anyone was ever more gifted with the English language, or any language for that matter—other than Christ himself and the writings inspired by his Spirit. So there is no way I can fully capture their eloquence, but I'll do my feeble best.

"I hope you didn't mind being greeted by my sister-in-law Georgina," Dickens said after she had ushered Spurgeon into his library, which was lined floor-to-ceiling by books on two sides, and by three large windows on another. Under the middle window sat a formidable desk, and above the author himself floated apparitions—not of his many characters like in the painting called "Dickens' Dream," but more good and bad spirits like those that accompanied his guest.

Apparently this was not just a unique meeting of two of the world's most famous men, but an important event in the spiritual realm also. Or maybe the forces of good and evil were always hard at work around both of them.

"I sent the servants away tonight," Dickens continued, "because I cannot necessarily trust them to keep confidence. Georgina, however, is quite discreet."

I could tell that Spurgeon reacted to this in his mind, thinking something to the effect of *I'm sure she is*, but saying nothing. The preacher didn't want to offend his new acquaintance at the very beginning of their meeting by hinting at the reports of the mistress who allegedly had ruined Dickens' marriage. (Most of the rumors swirled around a young actress named Ellen Tiernan, but there were also some less likely suspicions about Georgina, who since the separation had kept Dickens' house and cared for his ten children.)

Dickens, for his part, was only thinking this about Spurgeon: *He's shorter than I expected.*

I found even this partial awareness of the men's thoughts distracting and wanted to enjoy this visit as much as possible, so I asked my invisible companion if they could be "turned off." It must have worked, because from then on I could only hear the men's words.

"Should I call you Reverend?" Dickens asked, ushering the preacher to a chair across from his. "You don't seem to be the type for such affectations."

"I'm not," the burly younger man replied. "You can call me Charles."

"Wonderful. And you can call *me* Charles."

"Fast friends," Spurgeon said with a wry smile.

"And strange bedfellows?" Dickens responded.

"Perhaps not as strange as one might have thought," Spurgeon suggested, then pulled a note out of his pocket and held it up like a specimen.

2

"This invitation from you," the preacher said, "asks if I remember three recent donations of one thousand pounds each for our ministries, from an anonymous donor who had given only the initials A. B. So either you know the donor, or you are the donor."

"Forgive me for the intrigue," Dickens said. "'It was the only way I could assure you'd come tonight. From what I heard, those gifts arrived at a time of great need, so I was confident you'd want to express your appreciation in person."

"Great need is an understatement, my friend. The construction of our fledgling orphanage was halted until we received that first generous gift, and the second bank note from A. B. that arrived two weeks later put us ahead of schedule. You cannot imagine the rejoicing and praise to God, not to mention relief, those gifts solicited from our board and staff."

"I'm gratified," the famous author said, after a slightly embarrassed pause.

"I've had only the ride over here to make a guess at the meaning of the initials our anonymous donor chose."

"Oh? What do you suppose?"

"Anonymous Benefactor is the odds-on favorite," Spurgeon answered. "Or Admiring Benefactor perhaps. Or Angelo Bantam, the Master of Ceremonies in *The Pickwick Papers.*"

"I'm surprised that such an heir of the Puritans has a knowledge of gambling parlance, and I'm even more impressed that you would remember the name of a minor character from one of my novels."

"I remember everything I read," Spurgeon said, simply as a matter of fact, and with no visible pride. "So what *does* A. B. stand for?"

"Hmmm. I'm afraid you think me too clever. I simply picked the first two letters of the alphabet, seeing as the third and fourth might have given me away."

Both men laughed, and each did so with obvious sincerity. Even without the ability to read their minds or hearts, I could tell that neither was interested in making a show on this occasion.

"Speaking of *Pickwick*," Spurgeon added, "I've often said that my assistant George, whose given name is John L. Keys, reminds me of Sam Weller from that story. He certainly has many quaint sayings which that worthy might have uttered. You'd like him."

"I'm sure I would," Dickens said, and then grimaced from some kind of physical pain that was plaguing him.

"So the donations *were* from your hand," Spurgeon continued.

"If they were," Dickens admitted. "I'd be quite

obliged if you kept that between us."

"I certainly will, for I am the one obliged. I can't help but wonder at it, however. I never would have thought you to be an ally of mine."

"And I was not, until recently, when I found my mind to be opened."

"Why?" Spurgeon asked.

"Why was my mind opened, or why was I not an admirer of yours?"

"The latter first."

"Well, for one, your brand of Calvinism has always brought a particular stench to my nostrils. No pun intended."

"Perhaps because you misunderstand it," Spurgeon retorted. "It's nothing less than the absolute sovereignty of God over all, even evil—which I thought you illustrated well in your *Haunted Man* story."

"It may be nothing less, but it may also be something more—there's the rub, as The Bard might say. Which leads me to another reason you've rubbed me the wrong way (pun intended): you preach against the theater, which is actually my first love."

"I now understand why you were not an ally," Spurgeon said, "so I find it surprising that you did not become a public enemy by pointing your satirical bow in my direction."

"You've always seemed different, more worthy of respect, though not quite enough to escape your associations. Why have you not criticized *me* publicly?"

"For the same reason, though not quite enough to allay the suspicions."

"Ah," Dickens sighed, "the persistent gossip about my domestic difficulties. One thing I've learned in life is that no one but yourself will ever understand some things that befall you. I am not a perfect man by any means, but I assure you I am not as hideously monstrous as I am made out to be."

"I'm not inclined to disagree with you," the preacher said. "I myself don't happen to be as uncivil as some think. People often tell me that I'm more pleasant in person than in my sermons."

"But you seem to have more than narrowly avoided the disgrace and scandal that always seems to plague great men, whether deserved or not. Rather you are notorious for your devotion to an invalid wife."

"All glory be to God," Spurgeon said. "Though I often fail to love her as I should."

A moment of silence passed between the two men, indicating that they had reached the end of any discussion of the famous author's marital troubles. At least for now.

3

Then Spurgeon asked, "When did your mind open to the idea that I might not be a hypocrite like all the others?"

"When you announced that you were opening an orphanage in the vein of the Ragged Schools, which I have always supported."

"And a third bank note designated for our Pastors College," Spurgeon inquired further, "was delivered with the second donation to the orphanage, accompanied by a note saying, 'The latter led me to contribute to the former.'"

"Yes," Dickens explained. "I also became aware that you've been including people from other denominations in your various ministries, which clears you from another great fault I find with ministers of your ilk. And if you are able to seed the world with other men who will do the work you're doing, that may not be so bad after all, despite some of what you're teaching them."

"Let me guess," Spurgeon said. "You think that my care for the needs of the poor is happily inconsistent with my doctrines of original sin and total depravity?"

"I couldn't have said it better myself," Dickens responded.

"And I think, rather, that the two are unhappily consistent, because if those doctrines were not so true the needs would not be so great."

"I like to view the human race through rosier lenses."

"And I would love to do so, but I am not writing fiction and thus unable to create an alternate reality."

"Well, whether you are happily inconsistent or unhappily consistent," Dickens said, already beginning to tire of the still-young debate, "I am at least gratified that you shun what I call 'telescopic philanthropy.'"

"That I do," Spurgeon said. "I'm no Jellyby."

"And I shall reluctantly acknowledge that my most angelic characters are highly fictional."

"Well, now that we've very nearly missed establishing a Mutual Admiration Society," Spurgeon grinned, "why did you invite me to come tonight?"

"I wanted to ask you some questions, but I was shy of sending a letter."

"Yes, I understand you are given to burning them."

Dickens grimaced again, this time with a different kind of pain, and I initially wondered why his guest would be so rude as to break the unspoken policy of silence about the writer's possible infidelity. But then it occurred to me that Spurgeon may have been emulating the way Jesus related to the woman at the well in John 4, when He told her to call her husband and would not allow Himself to be diverted from the issue of her illicit relationships. Or this Baptist preacher may have felt conscience-bound to follow in the footsteps of John the Baptist, who was not intimidated in the presence of Herod the Great and refused to be silent about the King's affair with his sister-in-law. Or perhaps Spurgeon just imitated Jesus and John unconsciously, because he was so steeped in the Scriptures, and "if pricked would bleed Bibline," as he liked to say about his hero John Bunyan.

"Speaking of correspondence," Dickens said, clearing his throat in an apparent attempt to both shake off his pain and redirect the conversation, "This is what I wanted to ask you about."

He pulled two letters off his desk and held one out to Spurgeon.

"I received this today from the Reverend John Makeham," Dickens explained, "whose name I will refrain from mocking or using in one of my stories. As you can see, he takes exception to a sentence in the latest serialized chapter of *Edwin Drood*. Seems he thinks I was plagiarizing—and disparaging in some way—a passage from the Old Testament book of Isaiah. He implies that I was blaspheming our Lord, and since he is a Non-Conformist minister, I thought you could understand him better than I, and advise me."

"I don't conform to the Non-Conformists, and I dissent from most Dissenters," Spurgeon said without looking up from his perusal of the letter, "but I will be glad to help in any way I can."

"I fear that I am not long for this world," Dickens said, "and I'd prefer not to leave it in the midst of a religious controversy that could have been avoided. *Drood* might be my last work—I may not even be able to finish it."

"I'm sorry to hear about your health," Spurgeon said with genuine sympathy, meeting the writer's damp eyes. Then a small smile bent his lips ever-so-slightly, and he added, "But you *will* leave record of how the plot ends before you die, I hope…?"

It seemed to me that Spurgeon was not only a great preacher and leader, but also a good judge of personality. For far from being offended at this light-hearted spit in the Grim Reaper's eye, the legendary author actually warmed to it.

"Not a chance," Dickens answered. "After the initial frustration, my readers will have more fun with it if they don't know. The Boz's art has always imitated his mysterious life and will continue to do so even in death."

4

Dickens now held out his response letter to the Reverend Makeham and said that Spurgeon should read what he had written so far. The preacher took one look at the illegible handwriting, however, and suggested that Dickens read it for him. This elicited some more chuckles from both men.

"'Dear Sir,'" Dickens began, "'It would be quite inconceivable I think—but for your letter—that any reasonable reader could possibly attach a scriptural reference to a passage in a book of mine, reproducing a much-abused social figure of speech, impressed into all sorts of service on all sorts of inappropriate occasions, without the faintest connexion of it with its original source. I am truly shocked to find that any reader can make the mistake. I have always striven in my writings to express veneration for the life and lessons of our Saviour; because I feel it; and because I re-wrote that history for my children—every one of whom knew it from having it repeated to them—long before they could read, and almost as soon as they could speak.'"

"What do you think?" Dickens asked when he was done. "Will this mollify him and keep me from being dragged through the mud as a heretic among you—more than I've already been, that is?"

"Well," Spurgeon replied, "this Reverend Makeham might not recognize a metaphor if it bit him on the leg, but I think he will be more or less satisfied by the second half of the letter. You should not be so critical of him, however, because you bear some responsibility for his misapprehension of your words."

"How so?"

"You have not been clear and forthright enough in your profession of faith, especially in light of your frequent lampooning of religion. Even the book about Christ's life that you mention, which you wrote for your children, has never been released to the public."

"Bah!" the creator of Ebenezer Scrooge said, and I half-expected him to add "Humbug!" But he continued: "I've written other letters like this—I wish you could see them. But all right, I have ears to hear…"

Dickens swung his wheeled chair around, grabbed a pen, and grunted as he added one more line to the end of the letter, before signing it and folding it up.

(Later I found out what he wrote, because the letter has endured to the present day. The last line is, "But I have never made proclamation of this from the housetops." I also noticed, as Spurgeon had, how bad Dickens' handwriting was in the days prior to his death.)

When Dickens turned back to face his guest, Spurgeon sat quietly looking at him. A few moments of silence passed between the two men, and then the younger one broke it.

"There must be another reason you brought me here," Spurgeon said. "Something more grave than that letter. You haven't even offered me a drink or a cigar."

Dickens continued neglecting such hospitalities and examined the floor for a few more pregnant moments. Then he spun around again and retrieved a document from a drawer in his desk.

"This is my last will and testament," he said, "You shall tell me whether I've made a good end. I have wondered if I should modify it."

I sensed that Spurgeon was now starting to recognize the true nature of this pastoral call, and I was too.

The handwriting was much better on the will, having been done by an attorney, so the preacher took and read it as Dickens looked on, shifting occasionally in his seat from pain or nervousness or both.

"Whether or not you've made a good end of your *life*," Spurgeon said when he eventually handed the will back to Dickens, "is between you and the Lord. I cannot, nor can any man, be your judge in private matters such as your relationship with your wife and the other women you mention, unless you want to confide in me more about that. But I can say that you made a good end of the document itself."

"What do you mean?"

"Read the second-to-last sentence aloud, like a prayer."

"'I commit my soul to the mercy of God through our Lord and Saviour Jesus Christ, and I exhort my dear children humbly to try to guide themselves by the teaching of the New Testament in its broad spirit, and to put no faith in any man's narrow construction of its letter here or there.'" Dickens paused, then asked, "Is my disdain for denominations and theological arguments worthy of damnation?"

"Perhaps," Spurgeon answered with another wry smile. "All errors of doctrine are...even my own, whatever they might be. But you seem to have a desire to honor and obey God's Word, however deficient your understanding of it may be. Have you repented of your sins?"

"What precisely do you mean by 'repented'?"

"Repentance is a discovery of the evil of sin, a mourning that we have committed it, a resolution to forsake it. It is a change of mind of a very deep and practical character, which makes the man love what once he hated, and hate what once he loved."

Dickens pondered for a moment, then answered:

"There are many, ah, complexities that prevent me from knowing exactly what in my life has and has not been 'sin,' as you call it. I am a novelist, remember, not a priest. But I *am* sorry for whatever I've done wrong, what I know and what I do not."

"It may be that you have not knowingly repented of every sin you've committed," Spurgeon observed, "and you might not have produced all the commensurate fruits of repentance. I can only implore you to do so. But that leads us back to the first clause of that sentence. Read it again."

"'I commit my soul to the mercy of God through our Lord and Saviour Jesus Christ.'"

"Ahhh," Spurgeon said. "If that is truly the posture of your heart, I believe you can be confident of your justification and acceptance before God, regardless of how imperfectly you've repented or done anything else. I am not your confessor, nor can I absolve you or grant you assurance—only the Lord can do that. But I do find myself encouraged by the fact that your last words sound more like the tax collector than the Pharisee."

5

"I suppose you believe my christening as an infant to be unlawful," Dickens said. "and I must be baptized again?"

"Not if you must," Spurgeon replied.

After pausing for effect, the preacher elaborated: "If you feel that you must, I would fear that you were relying on your baptism rather than on Christ."

"Ah, you are referring to your most famous—or should I say notorious—sermon. 'On Baptismal Regeneration,' I think you called it."

"Yes, and one of my main points was that anyone who is resting upon baptism, or upon ceremonies of any sort, must shake off such venomous faith into the fire as Paul did the viper which fastened on his hand. As those two men praying in the temple illustrate, we are not saved because of who we are or what we have done, but because of *who Christ is* and *what He has done.*"

"I have in mind two other men," Dickens said. "Both of whom had something to say to Him in his last hours—and one of whom fared quite well afterward. So perhaps there is such a thing as a death-bed conversion."

The writer looked earnestly at the preacher, indicating that this was more of a question, and Spurgeon replied by quoting a hymn (one of his favorite pastimes):

    "The dying thief rejoiced to see
    That Fountain in his day
    And there may you, though vile as he,
    Wash all your sins away."

"On the other hand," Spurgeon added, "I heard that a physician once kept a record of a thousand persons who thought they were dying, and whom he thought were penitents. He wrote their names down in a book as those, who, if they had died, would go to heaven. They did not die, they lived; and he says that out of the whole thousand he had not three persons who turned out well afterwards, but they returned to their sins again, and were as bad as ever."

"Ha! I daresay." Dickens nodded. "So how could one know if he were a member of that microscopic minority?"

"Well, the very least thing that the Lord Jesus Christ can expect of us is that we confess Him to the best of our power. If you are nailed up to a cross, I will not invite you to be baptized. If you are fastened up to a tree to die, I will not ask you to come into my pulpit and declare your faith, for you cannot. But you are required to do what you can do, namely, to make as distinct and open an avowal of the Lord Jesus Christ as may be suitable in your present condition."

After a few moments, during which Dickens failed to ask for directions to the Metropolitan Tabernacle, Spurgeon added, "Besides, they would not baptize you again, or baptize you properly, in the kinds of churches you like."

"You might be surprised at some of the churches I have liked," the novelist said. "When I was nine and ten years old, my family often attended a Baptist Chapel similar to yours. I was taught—and not insignificantly influenced—by William Giles, the young adult son of the minister, and I was a playmate of his two younger brothers. I have visited Rusholme Chapel in Manchester, where my older sister Fanny assists her husband in directing the music, and my Uncle William attended Robert Street. I have never been an opponent of Dissent *per se*, nor have I been critical of any particular ecclesiastical stripe—only the false religion I see in any of them."

"The Jellybys and Collinses of the world?" Spurgeon said, and Dickens nodded again forcefully. "I'm glad to hear that, but I also would not want you to trust in a church any more than in a ceremony...

"No outward forms can make you clean,
The leprosy lies deep within...
Behold, I fall before thy face;
My only refuge is thy grace."

6

As there was another pause in the conversation, I noticed for the first time that the evil spirits had cleared out from the scene, and only elect angels were attending now. I didn't know whether this meant that Dickens was being converted or comforted, because the state of his soul was not apparent to me, or if the power of gospel truth had simply caused the darkness to flee. I found myself deeply hoping for one of the former.

"Would you pray for me?" Dickens said with tears in his eyes, though again I could not know their cause, whether it was joy or regret or both.

"I would love to," Spurgeon said, and took the writer's hands in his as he bowed.

"Our Father, Thou dost hear us when we pray. Thou hast provided an advocate and intercessor in heaven now; we cannot come to Thee unless Thy Holy Spirit shall suggest desire—and help us while we plead. We would ask that the subject which caused such conflict to Paul may be beyond conflict with us; may we know the Christ and have Him to be our all in all. We would have the conflict about others, but may we be past it for ourselves.

"Lord God the Holy Ghost, may faith grow in my friend Charles; may he believe in Christ to the saving of his soul. May his little faith brighten into strong faith, and may his strong faith ripen into the full assurance of faith. Resting in the Great Surety and High Priest of the New Covenant, may he feel 'the peace of God which passeth all understanding,' and may he enter into rest.

"May he not place his trust in his own good works of promoting charity for the poor, nor seek to excuse his sins by thinking he is not as corrupt as other men. May he not rely upon any words of mine, even the words of this prayer, but in Thy Word, O God—the only sure foundation upon which to build our house of faith. May these solemn words, which he has immortalized in his own writing, arise in his mind as he travels down the dark streets, among the heavy shadows: 'I am the resurrection and the life, saith the Lord: he that believeth in me, though he were dead, yet shall he live; and whosoever liveth and believeth in me, shall never die.'

"May this prayer that had broken up out of his heart for a merciful consideration of all his poor blindnesses and errors, end in the words, 'I am the resurrection and the life.' In his twilight may the substance of the shadow be apparent to him, may he take joy in the many lives that will be touched by the Divine truth he has put down, despite his sins and errors, and may he give Thee glory for any blessing that Thou mayest bestow through him.

"May he be able to say, in a humble faith that I hope and pray resides in his heart, 'It is a far, far better thing that I do, than I have ever done; it is a far, far better rest that I go to than I have ever known.' Amen."

Spurgeon opened his eyes and raised his head to see Dickens staring open-mouthed at him. The second half of the prayer had been filled with direct quotes from the end of his novel *A Tale of Two Cities*.

"I told you," the preacher said, "I remember everything I read."

****

The following morning, Charles Dickens sent out his response letter to the Reverend Makeham, and he spent that afternoon writing the next part of *The Mystery of Edwin Drood*. He suffered a massive stroke at dinner time, entering into a state of unconsciousness from which he would never recover, and died the next day.

The response to Makeham was Dickens' final letter, and on the last page he ever wrote (in the *Drood* manuscript) there is a funeral scene described in this way:

> A brilliant morning shines on the old city. Its antiquities and ruins are surpassingly beautiful, with a lusty ivy gleaming in the sun, and the rich trees waving in the balmy air. Changes of glorious light from moving

boughs, songs of birds, scents from gardens, woods, and fields—or, rather, from the one great garden of the whole cultivated island in its yielding time—penetrate into the Cathedral, subdue its earthy odour, and preach the Resurrection and the Life. The cold stone tombs of centuries ago grow warm; and flecks of brightness dart into the sternest marble corners of the building, fluttering there like wings.

Notes on the Story

<u>Notes on Chapter 1</u>

The opening quotation is from *The Pilgrim's Progress* by John Bunyan, a 17th Century pastor and author who was one of Spurgeon's biggest heroes. Spurgeon called that book "my great favorite" and read it over a hundred times. Bunyan's influence on Dickens can be seen in the full title of one of his most famous novels: *Oliver Twist, or The Parish Boy's Progress*. As a boy, Dickens attended a school run by a Baptist minister, where Bunyan's famous book was almost certainly required reading.

The fact that Dickens' sister-in-law Georgina sided with him in the dispute with his wife Catherine is considerable evidence that the marital situation was very complex and not just a simple case of adultery or abandonment on Dickens' part. Georgina seems to have been a woman of character who dearly loved the ten Dickens children (she cared for them for many years) and would not have supported them remaining with Charles unless there were significant problems in Catherine's life. That's not to say Charles wasn't to blame in various ways for the separation, or even primarily the cause of it, but as in most domestic conflicts, there was a lot more going on than outsiders realized.

"Dickens' Dream" is a painting by Robert William Buss, began shortly after Dickens' death and never finished because of the death of the artist himself. I have a rare canvas print of the painting hanging on the wall next to my home workspace.

Notes on Chapter 2

Here is the account, from Spurgeon's *Autobiography*, of the crucial donations that came in at the last possible moment to keep the orphanage project afloat:

> Many notable interpositions of Providence have occurred in connection with the building and maintenance of the Institution. One of the earliest and most memorable took place on November 20, 1867, concerning which Mr. Spurgeon wrote, several years afterwards, among his other personal recollections of Dr. Brock: — "We remember when, being somewhat indisposed, as is, alas! too often our' lot, we went to spend a

quiet day or two at a beloved friend's mansion in Regent's Park. We were dining, and Dr. Brock was one of our little company. Mention was made that the Stockwell Orphanage was being built, and that cash for the builder would be needed in a day or two, but was not yet in hand. We declared our confidence in God that the need would be supplied, and that we should never owe any man a pound for the Lord's work. Our friend agreed that, in the review of the past, such confidence was natural, and was due to our ever-faithful Lord. As we closed the meal, a servant entered, with a telegram from our secretary, to the effect that A. B., an unknown donor, had sent £1,000 for the Orphanage. No sooner had we read the words than the Doctor rose from the table and poured out his utterances of gratitude in the most joyful manner, closing with the suggestion that the very least thing we could do was to fall upon our knees at once, and magnify the Lord.... While we write the record, our heart wells up with new gratitude for the choice benefit. Surely, if in Heaven the saints shall converse together of the things of earth, this will be one of the subjects upon which two comrades of twenty years may be expected to commune." A few weeks later, the same anonymous donor dropped into the President's letter-box two bank-notes for £1,000 each, — one for the College, and the other for the Orphanage, — with a letter in which the generous giver said, "The latter led me to contribute to the former." This intimation was specially cheering to Mr.

Spurgeon for he had feared, perhaps naturally, that the new Institution would be likely to impoverish the older one.

There is no hint in the historical record, let alone any evidence, that Dickens made donations to Spurgeon's orphanage or college, but it's fun (and hopeful) to imagine such things in a fictional story.

Also from the *Autobiography*: "Mr. Spurgeon often said that George reminded him of Mr. Pickwick's Sam Weller, and he certainly had many quaint sayings which that worthy might have uttered."

Dickens' perspective on Calvinism seems to have been tainted by negative experiences he had with some people who advocated for that doctrinal perspective. In his book *God and Charles Dickens: Recovering the Christian Voice of a Classic Author*, Gary Colledge writes, "For whatever reasons, Dickens often portrayed the Dissenters and Noncomformists who embraced Calvinism as sullen and bad-tempered, and he attributed this to their misunderstanding of and an ungodly reversal in their religion. In *David Copperfield,* for instance, Mr. Murdstone and his sister are characterized by a religion which 'is a vent for their bad humours and arrogance.' Even more telling was that Murdstone 'gloomily profess[es]' his Christianity as he 'sets up an image of himself, and calls it the Divine Nature.'" (p. 7). In *Barnaby Rudge* Dickens refers to such professed Calvinists—not true ones, I would suggest—as "men of gloom and austerity, who paint the face of Infinite Benevolence with an eternal frown."

The idea that Dickens abandoned his wife for an adult-erous relationship is presented as fact by many con-temporary sources, like Claire Tomalin's book *The Invisible Woman* (along with the play and two movies inspired by it). But it's possible, given the facts that are known (and the number that are not), that both spouses were to blame for the breakdown of the marriage (Dickens retained sole custody of their ten children), and that the relationship with Ellen Tiernan stopped short of physical adultery (her mother was usually with them). If so, that's not to say the relationship wasn't inappropriate in various ways, but at least in Dickens' eyes he seemed to think it was not as bad as the rumor mill made it out to be, and by the end of his life he also seemed to be sorry for anything he had done wrong. This is all unproven conjecture, of course, but so is the assumption that he acted in the same scandalous way many celebrities do today—especially those who have no faith commitments.

As an example of the many evidences for Spurgeon's love for his wife Susannah, here is an excerpt from her own introduction to the *Autobiography*: "In 1868, my travel-ling days were done. Henceforth, for many years, I was a prisoner in a sick-chamber, and my beloved had to leave me when the strain of his many labors and responsibilities compelled him to seek rest far away from home. These separations were very painful to hearts so tenderly united as were ours, but we each bore our share of the sorrow as heroically as we could, and softened it as far as possible by constant correspondence."

Notes on Chapter 3

Spurgeon was a tireless, militant defender of the truth of the gospel, as has been well documented, and was probably too legalistic on some issues (e.g. the theater). But he also was rather ecumenical when it came to spiritual issues outside of the fundamentals of the faith. Consider this excerpt from the *Autobiography:* "The election of a Paedo-Baptist to such an important position was another instance of the catholicity of spirit that Mr. Spurgeon had manifested in appointing a Congregationalist (Mr. Rogers) to the post of Principal of the Pastors' College, and choosing another member of the same denomination (Mr. Selway) to be the Scientific Lecturer to that Institution. The undenominational character of the Orphanage is apparent from a glance at the table showing the religious views of the parents of the children received. Up to the date covered by the present volume, out of the 527 orphans who had found a happy home at Stockwell, no less than 166 had come from Church of England families, while Baptists were only represented by 121, Congregationalists by 64, Wesleyans by 58, and other bodies by still smaller numbers."

The term "telescopic philanthropy" and the character of Mrs. Jellyby are both from Dickens' novel *Bleak House*. Jellyby is so obsessed with starting a foreign mission in the African state of Borrioboola-Gha that she utterly neglects the needs of her own children and others around her.

For a discussion of Dickens' "angelic characters," among other interesting topics, see Keith Hooper's book *Dickens: Faith, Angels, and the Poor* (Lion Books, 2017).

We don't have Reverend Makeham's letter to Dickens, only a copy of Dickens' reply. However, we do have this extract from a letter by Makeham addressed to *The Daily News* soon after Dickens' death: "That the public may exactly understand the circumstances under which Charles Dickens's letter to me was written, I am bound to explain that it is in reply to a letter which I addressed to him in reference to a passage in the tenth chapter of 'Edwin Drood,' respecting which I ventured to suggest that he had, perhaps, forgotten that the figure of speech alluded to by him, in a way which, to my certain knowledge, was distasteful to some of his admirers, was drawn from a passage of Holy Writ which is greatly reverenced by a large number of his countrymen as a prophetic description of the sufferings of our Saviour." (From *The Letters of Charles Dickens,* Vol. 2 (of 3), 1857-1870, pp. 432-433.)

Notes on Chapter 4

For evidence of Dickens' bad handwriting, take a look at the Makeham letter itself:

Wednesday Eighth June 1870

Dear Sir

It would be quite
inconceivable to me - but for your
letter - that any reasonable reader
could possibly attach a scriptural
reference to a passage in a book
of mine, reproducing a much abused
social figure of speech impressed into
all sorts of service on all sorts of
inappropriate occasions, without the
faintest connexion of it with its
original source. I am truly
shocked to find that any reader can
make the mistake.

I have always striven in my
writings to express veneration for
the life and lessons of our Saviour;
because I feel it; and because I
re-wrote that history for my
children - every one of whom
knew it from having it repeated
to them - long before they could
read, and almost as soon as they could speak.

But I have never made
proclamation of this from the house tops.

Faithfully yours
Charles Dickens

John M. Makeham Esqre.

Dickens opposed the Temperance Movement because it advocated abstinence from all alcohol—he enjoyed various libations and favored moderation as the Christian approach. Spurgeon also initially opposed the movement, saying in his earlier years, "I am no total abstainer. I do not think the cure of England's drunkenness will come from that quarter" (quoted in Lewis Drummond, *Spurgeon: Prince of Preachers*, p. 380). But later in his life, after the events imagined in this story, he donned the "blue ribbon" of the Temperance Movement and advocated for abstinence. Regarding smoking, both Dickens and Spurgeon enjoyed cigars at this time, but Spurgeon gave them up later in life.

The book about Christ that Dickens refers to is *The Life of Our Lord*, a manuscript that he wrote for his children and personally read to them every year at Christmas time. The book begins: "My Dear Children, I am very anxious that you should know something about the History of Jesus Christ. For everybody ought to know about Him. No one ever lived who was so good, so kind, so gentle, and so sorry for all people who did wrong, or were in any way ill or miserable, as He was." One notable feature of the book is that Dickens recounted many of the miracle stories from the gospels and clearly believed they actually happened, which provides an important context for his visits to Unitarian churches. Dickens expressly told his family not to publish *The Life of our Lord*, and it was not released to the public until after all his children died.

Notes on Chapter 5

The quote about relying on baptism being "venomous faith" is almost word-for-word from Spurgeon's famous sermon "On Baptismal Regeneration." The quote about the two men in the temple (the Pharisee and tax collector from Luke 18:9-14) is one that I often repeat and like to think that Spurgeon would approve of.

In case someone might think that Spurgeon's words here are too positive regarding "death-bed conversions," following is a quote from his sermon "The Dying Thief in a New Light":

> I venture, however, to say that if I stood by the bedside of a dying man, tonight, and I found him anxious about his soul, but fearful that Christ could not save him because repentance had been put off so late, I would certainly quote the dying thief to him— and I would do it with good conscience—and without hesitation. I would tell him that, though he was as near to dying as the thief upon the cross was, yet if he repented of his sin and turned his face believingly to Christ, he would find eternal life. I would do this with all my heart, rejoicing that I had such a story to tell one at the gates of eternity! I do not think that I would be censured by the Holy Spirit for thus using a narrative which He has, Himself, recorded—recorded with the foresight that it would be so used. I would feel, at any rate, in my own heart, a sweet conviction that I had treated the subject as I ought to have treated it—and as it was intended to be used for men in extremis whose hearts are turning towards the living God. Oh, yes, poor Soul, whatever your age, or whatever the period of life to which you have come, you may now find eternal life by faith in Christ! [Spurgeon then quoted the hymn verse I put in the story.]

The story that Spurgeon tells about the physician and death-bed conversions is from "Confession of Sin–A Sermon with Seven Texts," and the paragraph about confessing Christ to the best of our power is a direct quote from the aforementioned sermon "The Dying Thief in a New Light."

When Spurgeon refers to the "churches you like," he means the Anglican churches of the Broad Church Movement that Dickens preferred and the Unitarian ones that the author sometimes visited. Those kinds of churches would not re-baptize someone who had been baptized as an infant, nor did they practice immersion as Spurgeon did.

In the story Dickens says, "I have never been an opponent of Dissent *per se*, nor have I been critical of any particular ecclesiastical stripe—only the false religion I see in any of them." This is well-argued and documented in Keith Hooper's doctoral dissertation *Dickens' Faith and His Early Fiction* (Chapter One), which was adapted into the book *Dickens: Faith, Angels, and the Poor.*

Spurgeon's reference to the "Collinses of this world" is a nod to the cringeworthy pastor from *Pride and Prejudice* by Jane Austen, whose works preceded these men and were appreciated by both of them. (Austen was the daughter of a conservative Anglican minister.)

The second hymn verse that Spurgeon quotes is from "Lord, I Am Vile, Conceived in Sin" by Isaac Watts. Spurgeon chooses this hymn partially because of Dickens' issues with the doctrine of original sin. Notice the first two verses:

Lord, we are vile, and full of sin,
We're born unholy and unclean;
Spring from the man whose guilty fall
Corrupts his race, and taints us all.

Soon as we draw our infant breath
The seeds of sin grow up for death;
Thy law demands a perfect heart,
But we're defiled in every part.

In Dickens' defense, his aversion to original sin was (and is) very common among compassionate people who have not studied much theology. And elsewhere he showed an appreciation for at least some of Isaac Watts' work—In *David Copperfied,* Dr. Strong (a generally sympathetic character) quotes favorably from a Watts poem about Satan making use of "idle hands."

Notes on Chapter 6

The first half of Spurgeon's prayer is adapted almost verbatim from sections of his recorded public prayers.

****

Following is some further proof that Spurgeon was familiar with Dickens, that he was not adversarial toward him, and that he even seemed to have some measure of respect for the famous author:

In Spurgeon's book *The Soul Winner,* the chapter titled "Sermons Likely to Win Souls" contains this illustration of the importance of good grammar for a preacher: "Did you ever hear how it was that Charles Dickens would not become a spiritualist? At a *séance,* he asked to see the spirit of Lindley Murray. There came in what professed to be the spirit of Lindley Murray, and Dickens asked, 'Are you Lindley Murray?' The reply came, '*I are.*' There was no hope of Dickens' conversion to spiritualism after that ungrammatical answer."

In Spurgeon's *Autobiography*, he replied in this way to students asking him about the value of reading fiction: "Some of Charles Dickens' works are worth reading, although he has given gross caricatures of the religious life of his times." (Vol. 4, p. 283)

The following not only proves Spurgeon's awareness of even obscure Dickens works, but also his long-term photographic memory: In an 1870 book called *Feathers for Arrows,* Spurgeon refers to a Dickens piece titled "The Last Cab-Driver" that was written *35 years previous* in 1835, the year after Spurgeon's birth!

In *The Salt Cellars Volume 1* Spurgeon actually records a saying by Dickens that cannot be found in any of the author's works:

> "Though house and land he never got,
> Learning will give what they cannot."

In *The Salt Cellars Volume 2* he writes, "When Charles Dickens heard an empty and pretentious young author declaiming against the follies and sins of the race, he remarked, 'What a lucky thing it is that you and I don't belong to it!'"

In Spurgeon's book *Eccentric Preachers,* the chapter on Edward Taylor opens with a quote from Dickens' *American Notes* about that particular preacher.

He began an 1869 article titled "Notes on Ritualism" in *The Sword and the Trowel* this way: "The Ritual Commission has issued its report, and with it a vast appendix. From amid dustheaps almost as huge as those which Dickens has immortalised, we have, by dint of riddling and using the sieve, extracted a few pieces of gold and silver, which we hope will pass for good metal and be as useful now as they were in the days long past."

An 1873 *Sword and Trowel* article titled "Language by Touch" starts with a reference to a deaf, dumb, and blind girl "whom Dickens saw in America, and so graphically described."

And in 1878, in a section of *Sword and Trowel* called "Notes," Spurgeon says, "As we walked through the quiet street in the afternoon, we were forcibly reminded of a chapter by Charles Dickens in his capacity as an 'Uncommercial Traveller,' in which he describes a visit to a similar, and, for aught we know, the same old coaching town." Spurgeon then reproduces a lengthy quote by Dickens about the town.

I am indebted to Phil Johnson, founder of Spurgeon.org and The Spurgeon Archives, for finding many of these references for me. Here is what Phil himself had to say about the two Charleses in a personal email:

> Spurgeon clearly read a lot of Dickens and did not hesitate to quote him. If they ever met, I don't think there's any record of it, but such a meeting might have taken place. Most people in London went to hear Spurgeon at least once. Several of Spurgeon's biographies mention the fact that many famous and powerful Londoners, including members of the royal family, came incognito to hear him. He wasn't one to drop names or boast about his connections with famous people, so Spurgeon himself would not necessarily have mentioned it if he met with Charles Dickens.

Haunted Man Preview

To experience a new version of a "forgotten classic" by Charles Dickens, which illustrates some of the profound spiritual truths championed by Charles Spurgeon, buy a copy of *Haunted Man* on Amazon, CruciformPress.com, or wherever books are sold.

The following pages contain a preview of the book…

**From Dave Swavely's introduction to *Haunted Man*,
written by Charles Dickens and abridged and annota-
ted by Swavely:**

These brief words will *not* ruin or lessen your enjoyment
of the following story in any way (I hate it when they do
that!); in fact, they will make you want to read it more and
will actually *increase* its pleasure and profit for you. So
please don't skip this introduction!

An argument can be made that *Haunted Man*—
especially this edition—is as good as *A Christmas Carol*,
though in a different way of course. But there is no doubt
whatsoever that the popularity of the latter (a beloved and
familiar classic) far exceeds the former (a neglected and
forgotten classic, but a classic nonetheless).

Why are so many familiar with *A Christmas Carol*,
but have never even heard of, let alone read, *The Haunted
Man and the Ghost's Bargain* (Dickens' original title)?
I'd like to suggest several reasons why this later novella
has been largely neglected and forgotten, and tell you how
this edition attempts to fix those problems. As I do, you'll
get a glimpse of why this book is truly a classic on the
level of Dickens' other great works, and you'll be pre-
pared to receive more enjoyment and edification as you
read it (with no spoilers, like I promised).

Watch the Language

As online reviews like those on GoodReads reveal,
some readers have difficulty with the wording of the
original Dickens story. It is common to hear complaints
about the unnecessary length of the story and the repeti-
tion of certain elements, which may or may not have
something to do with a required word count. And as is
always the case with Victorian literature, some of the
phraseology is simply not very intelligible to readers today.

Even though I'm a professional writer with a Master's

degree who loves Dickens, I myself had trouble following and staying with the story when I first encountered it, and I wasn't really blessed and moved by it until a second reading. So in preparing this version, I've done my best to help you to understand and enjoy it the first time you read it—or maybe *this* time if you've tried it before—by removing some of the wording that prevented me from appreciating it fully. I took out some sections and language that were unnecessary to the flow of the story and/or difficult to understand because of the century and a half between Dickens and us. I didn't add anything to the text, but simply removed about four thousand words here and there to make it run cleaner and smoother, like an updated engine in a classic car. I assure you that none of the abridgments change the basic meaning of any part of the story, and my commitment to make no additions or significant subtractions is illustrated by the fact that I retained Dickens' odd use of the phrase "D-n you!" at a key moment in the story. (He had guaranteed that there would be no vulgarity in his writing, so he had to use euphemisms and abbreviations to communicate certain emotions.)

We now have a version of this classic story that retains all the genius of Charles Dickens but makes it more accessible to modern audiences.

Bah Humbug!

A Christmas Carol was a huge hit when it was released in December of 1847, so it became a tradition for Dickens to publish a seasonal novella each year after that. *The Chimes* (1844) and *The Cricket on the Hearth* (1845) were very successful and well-reviewed, but then *The Battle of Life* (1846) was less so on both accounts, and Dickens took a break for a year before trying again with *The Haunted Man and the Ghost's Bargain* in 1848. By this time it was apparent that "the man who invented Christmas" had grown somewhat tired of repeating the formula of his most famous book, because although *Haunted Man* was marketed as another Christmas story, and contained many references to the holiday, it was not really that kind of story at all. One gets the impression that Dickens had an interesting tale he wanted to tell, and late 1848 just happened to be the best time for him to write and publish it. So he set the story at Christmas time, though it was totally unnecessary to the plot, and added in a number of extraneous yuletide references.

I've taken all but one of those references out for this abridged edition, to make it a "book for all seasons," which it deserves to be. As I said, the story is actually not about Christmas—it's more about the Cross, and some related theological and philosophical issues that a more mature Dickens wanted to explore. And I believe that such weighty themes are obscured in the minds of some readers by an incongruous association with *A Christmas Carol,* or with the holiday season in general.

A Christmas Carol works well as a holiday story because it's about the principle of "goodwill over greed" that is powerfully illustrated by The Nativity ("God so loved the world that he gave his only Son" when he was incarnated at Bethlehem). But *Haunted Man* is much more about The Passion ("God so loved the world that he gave his only Son" when he was sacrificed at Calvary). It's about a shocking irony of "theodicy"—the hard-to-swallow and even-harder-to-digest idea that God has a good purpose for allowing evil in our lives.

Dickens the Theologian?

I think that's another reason why *Haunted Man* is a forgotten classic. Some readers don't understand—and others won't accept—the theological and philosophical assumptions behind the plot. They don't necessarily agree with what Dickens says would happen if we were to lose all memory of past injuries and failures, because they don't like the idea that God has ordained them and therefore they must be (or at least they find that confusing and hard to grasp). In other words, some readers have probably been unsettled to discover that their beloved wordsmith believed in the absolute necessity of the Divine plan (including the existence of evil), and that in God's infinite wisdom it could have happened no other way.

Some readers also may not have appreciated how Dickens, who is commonly thought of as a nominal believer (at best), clearly implies that the solutions to our "problems with the past" lie in the death of Jesus Christ and the Divine grace we can receive from it.

I didn't remove those spiritual ideas from this abridged edition because they are taught in Scripture and therefore Christian readers, who are the primary intended audience, should be very open to them. And I hope that even those who are not committed Christians will thoughtfully consider them, as Dickens undoubtedly wanted us to do when he wrote the story.

May you enjoy this forgotten classic, and please continue on afterward to the Afterword, where spoilers are okay and I can discuss all of this in further detail.

About the Author

Dave Swavely is the author of numerous books, both fiction and non-fiction. His fiction includes the futuristic action/mystery Peacer series (*Silhouette* and *Kaleidocide*, published by Macmillan) and *Next Life* and *Haunted Man* (Cruciform Press). His non-fiction titles include *Life in the Father's House*, *Decisions Decisions*, *Who Are You to Judge?*, *From Embers to a Flame*, *Whole Counsel*, and *Unto Others: Rediscovering the Golden Rule*.

He has also edited many books by other authors and written numerous articles, songs, and poems, and has spoken at conferences throughout the country and abroad. He loves playing basketball, watching USC football, and reading graphic novels. He lives in beautiful Chester County, Pennsylvania with his wife of over 30 years, Jill, with whom he has raised seven children. He has been the founding pastor of three churches and the founding principal of two schools, has taught all ages of children for many years, and is President of the nonprofit ministry The Way With Words.

Dave's life journey has included many failures as well as successes, and he's learned the most from his failures.